Index

Author's Note

Preface

- Introduction to the Themes and Setting
- Background on the Characters
- Overview of the Story's Structure

Chapter 1: The Genesis of New Paths

- Final Semester Exams
- Campus Placements
- Plans and Aspirations

Chapter 2: A Reunion of Shadows

- Capturing Relations
- The Reunion Gathering
- Initial Signs of Supernatural Events

Chapter 3: Whispers from the Void

- Exploration of the Supernatural
- Rising Tensions Among Friends
- Early Confrontations and Revelations

Chapter 4: The Shattered veil

- Deepening Mysteries
- Increasing Conflicts and Struggles
- Heightened Supernatural Manifestations

Author's Note

Before You Begin:

Take a moment to reflect…

- Who do you trust the most in the world?
- Who holds your blind trust, without question or doubt?

Hold onto your answer as you journey through this story.

After Reading including "Epilogue":

Ask yourself:

- Has your answer changed?
- Do you still trust the same person, or has the story made you reconsider?

Feel free to share your Feedback or thoughts at saidurga52@gmail.com or on Instagram - @___son_of_krishna.

Preface

In the labyrinth of human consciousness, where shadows intertwine with the light, and where the boundaries between reality and imagination blur, lies the essence of our deepest fears and desires. ***THE REVOLT ON DECEPTION*** embarks on a journey through this enigmatic realm, exploring the consequences of our actions, the weight of our choices, and the supernatural forces that may manifest from our darkest corners.

This novel is not merely a tale of horror but a profound exploration of karma, redemption, and the intricacies of the human psyche. Through the lens of psychological and supernatural horror, we delve into the lives of characters grappling with their inner demons, the repercussions of their actions, and the ghosts of their past. Each chapter unveils layers of complexity, weaving a narrative that is as haunting as it is thought-provoking.

As you turn these pages, prepare to confront the deepest recesses of your own fears and beliefs. The story you are about to read is a reflection of the struggles and triumphs inherent in the human experience, shaped by the forces of fate and the echoes of choices made. Welcome to a world where the supernatural becomes a mirror to our inner selves, and where every action reverberates through the fabric of existence.

Chapter 1: The Genesis of New Paths

The sun cast a warm golden hue over the city of Tirupati as the final bell rang at Xavier's High School, signalling the end of another day. Students poured out of their classrooms, their chatter and laughter filling the air. Among them were Ananya and Chandra, two friends who had shared countless memories over the years.

Ananya stands out with her striking beauty and distinctive charm. Her thick, flowing hair frames a face, adorned with endearing dimples and large, expressive brown eyes that draw you in with their depth and warmth. The subtle addition of a bindi accentuates her unique look, making her presence both captivating and unforgettable. Ananya's appearance reflects her inner grace and confidence, blending elegance with a touch of personal style. Yet, beneath that fierce drive, there was a warmth that made her approachable, a kindness that drew people to her.

Chandra, on the other hand, was quieter, more introspective. He exudes a distinct presence with his clear jawline and sharp, intense eyes. His silky hair falls effortlessly over his face, adding to his striking and captivating appearance. His deep-set eyes often seemed to be lost in thought, as if he were constantly pondering the mysteries of life.

Chandra first noticed Ananya during a visit to Vizag Beach with his friends. Ananya was there with her parents, and he recognized her from school, though they hadn't spoken much before. As she struggled with a red heart-shaped balloon that slipped from her grasp, Chandra swiftly caught it and returned it to her. Their shared smiles marked the beginning of a connection. This brief but meaningful encounter led to their first conversations at school. As their discussions grew deeper each day, they began to share more of their personal lives with each other. Over time, their bond strengthened, fostering a deep trust and a meaningful friendship.

The school library, usually bustling with students, was unusually quiet that afternoon. Ananya and Chandra had found their usual spot near the back, surrounded by shelves that seemed to reach the ceiling. Ananya was buried in her textbook, her brow furrowed in concentration, while Chandra methodically made notes in his notebook.

Today, however, there was an unspoken weight in the air, a sense that their time at school was drawing to a close. Breaking the silence, Ananya sighed and looked up from her book. "Chandra, do you ever wonder what's next? Like, after school?" Her voice was thoughtful, tinged with a rare vulnerability.

Chandra paused, his pen hovering over the paper. He met her gaze, his expression serious. "I think about it all the time. It's overwhelming, isn't it? But I believe as long as we keep supporting each other, we'll figure it out."

Ananya smiled, a genuine warmth spreading across her face. "You always have a way of making things seem less scary. I'm glad I have you as a friend, Chandra."

Chandra returned her smile, feeling a surge of affection for his friend. "I'm grateful for you too, Ananya. You push me to be better, to aim higher."

Their words hung in the air, a silent promise to each other that whatever came next, they would face it together.

On their first day of college, the sprawling campus was alive with energy as students hustled between classes, finding their rhythm in this new chapter of their lives. Chandra and Ananya, true to their promise, stuck together, and their bond only grew stronger. Yet, the college environment also hinted at the possibility of new connections and experiences.

As days passed by, one sunny afternoon, after a gruelling lecture, Chandra and Ananya decided to unwind in the college library. As they were leaving, Ananya noticed a boy sitting alone under a large tree in the courtyard, his focus entirely on the notebook in his lap. He was scribbling furiously, lost in his thoughts.

"Who's that?" Ananya asked, nudging Chandra.

Chandra followed her gaze and recognized the boy as Bharat, a classmate known for his carefree attitude and sense of humour. "That's Bharat. He's always got some crazy story or joke up his sleeve. A bit of a clown, but in a good way."

Ananya smiled, intrigued by Bharat's intense focus despite his reputation for humour. "Let's go talk to him."

As they approached, Bharat looked up and flashed a wide grin. "Hey, Chandra! Ananya! You guys want to hear something wild?"

Before they could respond, Bharat launched into an animated retelling of a Funny story he had recently heard. His expressive face and exaggerated gestures were captivating, pulling Chandra and Ananya into the tale. They found themselves laughing uncontrollably, their earlier fatigue forgotten.

Ananya, wiping tears of laughter from her eyes, said, "You're hilarious, Bharat. We should hang out more often."

Chandra nodded, surprised at how quickly he felt comfortable around Bharat. "Yeah, join us for lunch tomorrow?"

Bharat's grin widened. "Count me in!"

Over the next few weeks, Bharat became a regular part of their group. His easy-going nature and infectious humour brought a new dynamic to their friendship, making their days on campus more vibrant and unpredictable.

As the trio grew closer, their daily routines on campus became more intertwined. One afternoon, they decided to grab coffee at the campus café, a favourite spot for students to unwind and engage in spirited debates.

As they settled into their seats, they couldn't help but overhear a heated discussion at the table next to them. A tall, lanky boy with wild hair was passionately defending the merits of horror movies to a group of sceptical students. His eyes gleamed with excitement as he described the latest horror flick he had watched.

Bharat leaned in and whispered to Ananya and Chandra, "That's Rakesh. He's obsessed with horror and ghosts. A bit intense, but he's got some good stories."

Ananya, always up for a lively conversation, leaned over to Rakesh. "Hey, mind if we join the debate?"

Rakesh looked up, surprised but pleased by the interest. "Sure, the more, the merrier! But be warned, I take my horror seriously."

What started as a casual debate turned into a spirited discussion that lasted over an hour. Rakesh's deep knowledge and enthusiasm for all things horror intrigued the group, adding a unique flavour to their conversations. By the end of it, Rakesh was thoroughly integrated into their circle, his passion for the macabre making their interactions even more interesting.

A few months passed, and the group's bond grew stronger. Each day brought new experiences and deeper connections. It was during this time that a new face began to turn heads on campus.

Isha, with her modern, stylish flair, quickly became a topic of conversation among the students. Her confidence and unique fashion sense made her stand out in any crowd. One day, as Ananya was leaving her class, she accidentally bumped into Isha at the entrance.

"Sorry!" Ananya said, steadying herself.

"No problem," Isha replied with a warm smile. "I'm still getting used to this place."

Ananya noticed a fashion magazine peeking out of Isha's bag. "You're into fashion?"

Isha's eyes lit up. "Yes! I'm actually planning to attend a fashion show in Mumbai this weekend."

Ananya's interest was piqued. "That sounds amazing! We should grab coffee sometime. I'd love to hear more about it."

Isha agreed, and soon after, she became the newest member of their group. Her modern outlook and passion for fashion added yet another layer to the diverse personalities that made up their circle. Isha's admiration for Bharat's carefree attitude and love for life also started to show, slowly weaving new threads into the fabric of their friendship.

The café, a popular hangout spot, was a familiar and comforting refuge for the group.

One day, As Chandra and Ananya entered the café, they were greeted by Bharat's infectious laughter and Rakesh's animated storytelling. The café was alive with the chatter of students and the aroma of freshly brewed coffee.

Bharat, with his free-spirited attitude and easy humour, was in the middle of a story. His animated gestures and expressive face drew the attention of everyone around him. Rakesh, ever the horror enthusiast, was leaning in, clearly intrigued by Bharat's tale.

"...and then," Bharat continued with a flourish, "The ghost just vanished into thin air! Can you believe that?"

Rakesh's eyes widened with excitement. "That's incredible! I have to hear more about this. It's just the kind of thing I'd love to include in one of my horror stories."

Ananya and Chandra took their seats at the table, joining in the lively conversation. Ananya, always ready with a witty comment, turned to Bharat with a smirk. "You know, Bharat, your stories are always entertaining, but I'm not sure if I'll ever be brave enough to go ghost-hunting with you."

Bharat grinned, clearly enjoying the banter. "Oh, come on, Ananya! You wouldn't want to miss out on all the fun. Besides, you might just end up being the hero of the story!"

Chandra, who had been quietly observing, decided to chime in. "Or we could just stick to less terrifying adventures, like finding the best coffee in town. What do you think, Rakesh?"

Rakesh laughed, shaking his head. "That sounds like a plan. But I promise, my ghost stories will still be the highlight of our hangouts."

As the group continued to chat, "Hey, everyone!" Isha greeted, her eyes sparkling with excitement. "What's the latest on the ghost-hunting front?"

Bharat's face lit up as he welcomed Isha into the conversation. "Just telling Rakesh about my latest ghost story. You should join us on one of our adventures sometime."

Isha laughed gently, "Count me in. I love a good adventure, especially if it involves a bit of excitement."

As the afternoon wore on, the café was filled with laughter and animated conversations. The group's bond was evident in their easy camaraderie and playful exchanges. The mix of personalities—Ananya's ambition, Chandra's thoughtfulness, Bharat's humor, Rakesh's fascination with horror, and Isha's vibrant energy—created a dynamic that was both engaging and enjoyable.

The café became their haven, a place where they could escape the pressures of college life and simply enjoy each other's company. Friendship which forged in the fires of school and strengthened in college, was a testament to the power of connection and the joy of shared experiences.

The sun dipped low in the sky as Ananya and Chandra walked side by side through the bustling college campus. They had been friends since school, their bond as solid as the oak tree they often sat beneath. Ananya, with her graceful demeanour and sharp intellect, was admired by many, but it was her kindness that had always drawn Chandra to her. He had known her for so long that he could read the unspoken thoughts behind her calm expressions.

Their footsteps echoed softly in the quiet of the evening, the fading light casting long shadows on the path.
"Time's slipping away faster than I thought," Ananya mused, her voice carrying a hint of wistfulness.

The golden hues of the setting sun caught in her brown eyes, making them appear even more luminous.

Chandra glanced at her, a gentle smile tugging at his lips. "It feels like we blinked, and suddenly, we're here—on the cusp of something new and terrifying."

Ananya laughed, a light, musical sound that made Chandra smile wider. But as they continued walking, a thought lingered in his mind—Bharat. He had noticed how Ananya's laughter seemed to brighten whenever Bharat was around, and how her gaze lingered a little longer when she looked at him.

Bharat, with his easy-going charm and infectious sense of humour, had a way of making everyone feel at ease. He was the kind of person who could turn the most mundane moment into something memorable. And lately, Chandra had seen a subtle change in the way Ananya interacted with him—a softness, a warmth that hadn't been there before.

The next day, the group gathered at their usual spot in the campus café. Rakesh animatedly recounted a real-life event that took place at his aunt's house in her village. It all began when his aunt went to the bazaar and a quarrel broke out, escalating over the days.

Eventually, black magic was used against her. He vividly remembers the day his aunt, bedridden and feeling ill, seemed to be lifted from her bed, a feet high. she floating in a trance , like state with pins on her forehead and hands causing severe pain even though there were none. She cried out, claiming that a man on the beach, was performing black magic on her, with a doll prepared just like her with her hair and piece of her cloth and urging them to stop him immediately. When his uncle investigated, they found someone who was actually performing the ritual at the shore which is actually 20km away, they immediately stooped the guy and took control.

That was when i began to believe in the supernatural.

As Rakesh animatedly recounted the eerie events at his aunt's village, Isha, lost in thoughts imagining his narration.

As the conversation flowed, Bharat leaned closer to Ananya, who was sitting beside him. "Hey, did you finish that book I recommended?" he asked, his voice just above a whisper, as if the rest of the world didn't matter in that moment.

Ananya smiled, her eyes meeting his. "I did. It was amazing. I couldn't put it down."

Their exchange didn't go unnoticed by the others. There was a subtle, almost imperceptible shift in the atmosphere—a newfound connection between Ananya and Bharat that was slowly blossoming.

Over the next few weeks, the two spent more time together, often studying late into the night in the college library or grabbing coffee during breaks. They shared conversations that ranged from their dreams and aspirations to the little quirks that made them who they were.

One day, as the group was hanging out in the café, Bharat mentioned that he had to go back to his native place for a couple of weeks. "I haven't been home in a while," he said casually, though his gaze lingered on Ananya. "I'll be leaving this weekend."

Ananya's heart sank at the thought of him leaving, even if just for a short while. She forced a smile, trying to hide her disappointment. "That's good. You'll get to spend time with your family."

But that night, as Ananya lay in bed, the thought of Bharat leaving overwhelmed her. Tears welled up in her eyes, surprising her with their intensity. She hadn't realized just how much she had grown attached to him, how his presence had become something she relied on.

When Bharat left for his hometown, Ananya felt an emptiness she couldn't quite explain. The days felt longer, and the usual activities she enjoyed seemed dull. She missed their late-night study sessions, their coffee breaks, and the way he made her laugh.

Bharat, too, felt the distance. Every evening, he would find a quiet corner in his parents' house to text Ananya, sharing the details of his day as if he were still with her. "I went for a walk by the lake today," he wrote one night. "It reminded me of that time we skipped class and went to the park."

Ananya smiled at the memory as she read his message, her heart-warming at the thought that he was thinking of her, too. Their chats became a nightly ritual, a lifeline that kept them connected despite the miles between them.

One evening, after a long day, Bharat sent a message that made Ananya's heart skip a beat. "I miss you," he typed, his words simple but filled with meaning.

Ananya stared at the screen, her fingers hovering over the keys. Finally, she replied, "I miss you too."

When Bharat returned to college, their bond was stronger than ever. The time apart had made them realize just how much they meant to each other, and though neither had openly confessed their feelings, there was an unspoken understanding between them. They were more than just friends now, and both of them knew it.

As the final semester approached, the group faced the challenges of exams and placements. The once carefree days of college were now filled with the stress of securing their futures.

The café, once filled with lively conversations, was now quieter, as each of them focused on their studies. But even in the midst of all this, Ananya and Bharat found moments to share a smile, a glance, a touch that reassured them of each other's presence.

One afternoon, as they gathered in the library, Ananya spoke up, breaking the silence. "I've decided to pursue further studies after college," she said, her voice steady but tinged with the uncertainty of the unknown. "It's going to be tough, but I'm excited about the possibilities."

Chandra nodded, admiring her determination. "That sounds great, Ananya. I'm heading to Hyderabad for my job. It's a big step, but I'm ready for it."

Rakesh, who had been flipping through pages of a horror novel, chimed in, "And I'm off to Vizag with Bharat. It's going to be a change, but I'm looking forward to it."

Bharat grinned, his easy-going nature shining through. "Absolutely! Vizag has its charm. Besides, Isha's regular trips to Mumbai for her fashion shows will give us a chance to explore both cities."

Isha, who had been quietly listening, smiled at the mention of her name. "Yes, I'll be commuting to Mumbai, but it's worth it for my passion. I can't wait to dive into the fashion scene."

The friends exchanged glances, a mix of excitement and nostalgia washing over them. Their paths were diverging, each of them setting out on their own journey, but the bond they shared would remain, a constant in their ever-changing lives.

As they prepared for their final exams, the weight of what lay ahead began to settle in. The late-night study sessions were no longer just about passing tests but about preparing for the next chapter of their lives. They supported each other through the stress, sharing notes, offering words of encouragement, and sometimes just sitting together in comfortable silence, knowing they were not alone in this.

The day of the last exam arrived, marking the end of an era. As they walked out of the exam hall, the reality of it all hit them. This was it—their college days were officially over. There was a sense of accomplishment, but also a tinge of sadness, knowing that things would never be the same again.

After the exams, they spent their remaining days on campus reminiscing about the past few years. They revisited their favourite spots, from the tree where Ananya and Chandra had spent countless hours, to the café where they had laughed and shared stories. It was a bittersweet time, filled with laughter, tears, and the unspoken understanding that they were all stepping into a new world.

The day finally came when they had to part ways. Standing at the train station, they hugged each other tightly, not wanting to let go.

"Keep in touch, okay?" Ananya said, her voice cracking as she hugged Bharat.

"Of course," Bharat replied, his eyes glistening. "We'll see each other soon."

Chandra gave them all a reassuring smile. "This isn't goodbye. It's just the beginning of new paths for all of us."

Rakesh, always the optimist, added, "And we'll have our reunion soon. Maybe at a haunted house or something," he joked, trying to lighten the mood.

Isha laughed, wiping away a tear. "Count me out of the haunted house, but I'm in for anything else."

With that, they each boarded their respective trains, heading towards their futures. As the train pulled away, they waved at each other, their faces a mixture of hope, excitement, and the sadness of leaving behind the place where they had grown up together.

The memories of their time together would always remain, a chapter of their lives that had shaped them into who they were. They were now ready to face the world, armed with the knowledge that no matter where life took them, they would always have each other.

Chapter 2: A Reunion of Shadows

The days after their departure were bittersweet. Ananya and Bharat, now separated by miles, found solace in the nightly ritual of texting each other. What started as casual check-ins quickly became a lifeline, a thread that kept them connected despite the distance. But as time went on, the longing grew, and so did the complexities of their relationship.

Ananya would often stare at her phone, waiting for Bharat's message, her heart skipping a beat whenever his name flashed on the screen. They would talk about their day, share the little moments that made them smile, and sometimes just exchange random thoughts that kept them close. But the distance wasn't easy. There were days when Bharat would post a photo with his colleagues, a casual arm around a female friend, and a wave of possessiveness would wash over Ananya.

"Who's that girl in the picture?" Ananya would ask, trying to keep her tone light but failing to hide the edge in her voice.

"Oh, that's just a colleague," Bharat would reply, sensing the tension. "We were out for lunch after a meeting. It's nothing."

But the seed of doubt had been planted, and it would often lead to late-night quarrels. The arguments were never about the actual issue, but rather about the distance that made every small thing feel amplified. Ananya would sometimes cry herself to sleep, feeling silly for letting her insecurities get the best of her.

However, Bharat always knew how to make things right. He would apologize, not just with words but with sincerity that melted Ananya's heart. "I'm sorry, Ananya," he would text or sometimes call late at night. "You're the only one I care about. I miss you so much."

And every time, Ananya would forgive him. The love they had for each other only grew stronger with each challenge, as if the distance was a test they were determined to pass. They would plan their next meet-up, counting down the days until they could be together again.

Their first reunion was eagerly anticipated by both of them. They decided to meet at Punyagiri, a serene location known for its beautiful waterfall and the temple of Lord Shiva. It was a place that held a special charm, perfect for their much-needed escape from the world.

The day of the meetup was overcast, the sky heavy with clouds threatening rain. They met at the base of the temple, their eyes lighting up at the sight of each other. Bharat pulled Ananya into a tight hug, feeling the warmth of her body against his after what felt like an eternity.

"I missed you so much," he whispered into her hair, his voice filled with emotion.

"I missed you too," Ananya replied, holding him close, as if afraid he might disappear if she let go.

They explored the temple, offering their prayers, and then made their way to the waterfall. The air was thick with the smell of wet earth as the first drops of rain began to fall.

What started as a light drizzle quickly turned into a downpour, drenching them both.

Completely soaked, they decided to book a nearby hotel for the night. The room was simple but cozy, with a large window that offered a view of the rain-soaked landscape. They took turns freshening up, the warm water of the shower a welcome relief from the cold rain.

Later, they settled on the bed, snuggled up under a blanket, and decided to watch an episode of *Game of Thrones* on Bharat's laptop. The storm outside raged on, but inside, there was a growing tension of a different kind.

As the episode played on, Bharat couldn't focus. His attention kept drifting to Ananya, who was lying close to him, her body warm and soft against his. He could feel his heart beating faster, a mix of nervousness and desire.

Without thinking, Bharat leaned over and kissed her gently on the lips. Ananya responded, her lips soft and inviting, as if they had been waiting for this moment. The kiss deepened slowly, their tongues meeting and intertwining in a dance that was both tender and passionate, exploring each other with a yearning that had been simmering beneath the surface for months.

Bharat's hand moved instinctively, tracing the curve of her waist, his fingers brushing against her skin as if it were the most delicate thing he'd ever touched. Ananya's breath caught in her throat, her heart racing as his touch sent shivers down her spine. She hesitated for a brief moment, her voice barely a whisper, "Stop…" But her body told a different story, her breath quickening, her pulse throbbing with a need that had long been denied.

Bharat felt her surrender and continued, his touch growing more confident, more assured. He explored her body with a reverence that made Ananya feel cherished, desired in a way she had never experienced before. Every caress, every kiss, was an unspoken promise, a testament to the love they had nurtured despite the miles that had separated them.

Ananya moaned softly, her hands finding their way to Bharat's body, mirroring his tenderness with her own. Their touches became more urgent, more desperate, as if they were trying to make up for all the time they had spent apart. The room seemed to shrink around them, the outside world fading away until all that existed was the two of them, wrapped in each other's arms.

Bharat kissed her again, deeper this time, his tongue teasing hers as he explored her mouth with a hunger that had been building for so long. His lips lingered on hers as his hands roamed freely, exploring every inch of her. He kissed her neck, her collarbone, moving slowly, savouring every moment as if he were memorizing her, committing every curve and contour to memory. Ananya's fingers tangled in his hair, pulling him closer, wanting more, and needing more.

As their bodies came together, the passion that had been simmering for so long finally erupted, consuming them both in a wave of emotion that left them breathless. They moved in perfect harmony, their bodies perfectly attuned to each other, as if they had been made for this very moment.

But just as quickly as it had begun, it was over. Bharat climaxed almost instantly, his orgasm intense but brief, leaving him embarrassed and apologetic as he realized he had lasted mere seconds.

Ananya, her own pleasure unfulfilled, quickly got up and went to the bathroom. She cleaned herself, her mind racing with thoughts of preventing pregnancy. The reality of what had just happened began to sink in as she splashed water on her face, trying to calm herself.

When she returned to the room, Bharat was lying on the bed, staring at the ceiling, a mix of regret and satisfaction on his face. Ananya crawled back under the blanket with him, her hand finding his.

"I'm sorry," Bharat whispered, his voice heavy with guilt.

Ananya smiled softly, squeezing his hand. "It's okay. We'll figure it out."

And they did it again. Over the next few months, they met up frequently, their bond growing deeper with each encounter. They visited different places together, from quiet temples to bustling cities, exploring not just the world around them but each other as well. Their physical relationship became a natural extension of their emotional connection, the two of them learning to navigate the complexities of love, desire, and intimacy.

Despite the ups and downs, the fights, and the misunderstandings, Bharat and Ananya found a way to make their relationship work. The distance no longer felt like an obstacle but a challenge they had overcome together. And with each new experience, their love grew stronger, a bond that would withstand whatever the future had in store for them.

On the other side, the group of five kept in constant touch through their WhatsApp group, which they had cheekily named "Indestructible Tribes" This virtual hangout was where they shared updates, jokes, and memories. Bharat, ever the adventurer, often made trips to Mumbai with Isha, eager to experience the city's vibrant life alongside her.

Rakesh, always the horror enthusiast, balanced his love for the eerie with the harsh realities of his financial situation. Despite his struggles, he remained determined to make something of himself. Rakesh often joining Bharat in his explorations and adventures and even began exploring loan options through various apps, hoping to ease his burden and enjoy life a little with the money he secured.

Meanwhile, Chandra found himself increasingly drawn into the darker side of city life. Surrounded by temptations and negative influences, his inner demons began to take hold. His overthinking tendencies and hidden vices started to fester, pushing him further into a world of internal conflict.

As Chandra's birthday approached, he eagerly called for a get-together at a resort, planning a reunion that promised to be a night of celebration and nostalgia. The friends gathered with a sense of excitement, the air thick with anticipation as they prepared to catch up, share stories, and relive old memories.

The evening started off joyfully. Drinks flowed freely, and the group settled into a relaxed atmosphere, eventually deciding to play a game of truth or dare. Laughter filled the room as the dares became increasingly bold, and the truths more revealing. The carefree mood, however, took a turn when Bharat and Isha offered to go downstairs to fetch more drinks.

A few minutes later, Ananya, feeling a need to help out, followed them. But as she approached, something caught her eye—a scene that shattered her world in an instant. Hidden in the shadows, she saw Bharat and Isha, their bodies pressed together in a passionate embrace. Bharat had Isha pinned against the wall, one of her legs draped over his shoulder as they kissed and made love.

Ananya froze, her breath catching in her throat as disbelief washed over her. Her mind raced, struggling to comprehend the betrayal unfolding before her eyes. Bharat, the one person she had trusted above all others, was entangled with Isha in a moment of intimacy that broke her heart.

Without a word, Ananya turned and slipped away, retreating to her room in a silent storm of shock and anguish. Tears welled up as she tried to process the scene she had witnessed. Alone in the quiet of her room, Ananya cried in silence, her world crumbling around her. The love and trust she had cherished so deeply were shattered, and the pain was more than she could bear and quietly returned to the hall, holding the sorrow deep in her heart.

When Bharat and Isha returned with the drinks, the others were unaware of the storm brewing within Ananya. She excused herself quietly, her tears flowing freely as she grappled with the unbearable truth. Unable to contain the whirlwind of emotions, she slipped out onto the terrace, hoping the night air might somehow soothe her aching heart.

The night was dark, the sky void of stars, as if even the heavens had turned away from her pain. A few seconds later, Bharat, noticing her absence, followed her to the terrace, unaware of the turmoil raging within her. Isha watched silently from a distance, her expression unreadable.

When Ananya saw Bharat stepping onto the terrace, she quickly composed herself, forcing a smile as she greeted him. "Hey, Bharat," she said, her voice calm, almost too calm. "How's everything in Mumbai? You've been there so often lately. What places have you explored?"

Bharat, not suspecting anything, leaned against the railing beside her, oblivious to the storm brewing beneath her facade. He started talking about his recent trips to Mumbai, mentioning the vibrant streets, the food, and the places he had visited. He spoke casually, recounting his adventures without a second thought.

As Bharat spoke, Ananya listened intently, her mind racing as she connected the dots. Each word he said felt like a dagger twisting in her heart. The memories of their past conversations, his unexplained absences, and his frequent trips to Mumbai now made perfect, painful sense. All this time, she had been blind to the truth, fooled by the very person she had trusted the most.

Ananya kept her expression neutral, nodding along to Bharat's stories, but inside, she was screaming. The realization that she had been deceived, that her love and trust had been taken for granted, was almost too much to bear. Yet, she continued to ask questions, her tone light and curious, all the while masking the devastation within her.

As Bharat finished his tales of Mumbai, Ananya felt a hollow ache in her chest. She had all the answers she needed now. Her suspicions were confirmed, and the truth was bitterer than she had ever imagined. She managed to keep her composure, not letting Bharat see the cracks in her facade. But inside, she was breaking apart, piece by piece.

Chandra, slightly tipsy, was lounging on a couch, the effects of the alcohol softening his usual guarded demeanour. Rakesh, meanwhile, was chatting with his sister using Bharat's phone since his network was weak.

Anxious and worried about what might be unfolding between Ananya and Bharat on the terrace, Isha decided to take Chandra and Rakesh upstairs. The cool night air and the buzz of alcohol seemed to infuse a new energy into the group. Chandra, ever the host, enthusiastically mixed a round of drinks, determined to keep the evening lively and engaging.

Isha couldn't ignore the sight of Ananya and Bharat together. Her jealousy flared up, feeding into her negative thoughts. She masked her irritation well enough at first, but the emotions were like a ticking time bomb, waiting to explode. When the night wound down, the group retired to their rooms, and Ananya found herself sharing a room with Isha.

As the night deepened and the house fell into a quiet lull, Ananya and Isha found themselves alone in the dimly lit room. The silence stretched between them, heavy with the weight of unspoken tension. Ananya, her heart pounding with a mix of frustration and anxiety, finally broke the silence.

"Isha," she began, her voice cutting through the stillness like a knife, "what exactly are your feelings for Bharat?"

The question hung in the air, charged with a tension that seemed to crackle with each breath. Isha's eyes flashed with hurt and anger. Her emotions, already frayed by the evening's events, surged uncontrollably. "What does it matter to you, Ananya? Do you think you're the only one who can love him? Just because you're with him doesn't mean you own him!"

Ananya's face flushed with a mix of embarrassment and fury. "This isn't about ownership! Bharat and I—" Her voice cracked, "We have a history, and it's not something you can just barge into and expect to take over!"

The argument, once simmering beneath the surface, erupted into a full-blown confrontation. Isha's eyes narrowed, her voice dripping with scorn. "Is that what you think? That I'm just trying to take something from you? You think you're so superior, so untouchable?"

Harsh words and bitter accusations flew back and forth, each one hitting with painful accuracy. Isha angrily said, "It was Bharat who first came to me, seduced me, even when he had you. I know you two are together, but we had more than just you. He wants me, not you Ananya. You are nothing." The tension between them was palpable, and their anger only intensified their heated exchange. Ananya's hands trembled as she gestured wildly, her face a mask of frustration.

In a moment of uncontrolled rage, Ananya's hand struck Isha across the face with a loud slap. The sound echoed through the room, and before Isha could fully react to the shock, she retaliated with a wild, desperate shove.

The struggle between them quickly escalated. They grappled, their movements frantic and uncontrolled. Each jab and shove was laced with their pent-up emotions—pain, betrayal, and envy. The room, once quiet and serene, became a battleground of raw, unfiltered emotions.

In their heated clash, their voices became incoherent cries, their movements a blur of anger and desperation. It was as if they were locked in a fierce dance of fury, with each attempting to overpower the other. The struggle grew more intense, with both women losing their grip on control.

Amid the chaos, the world seemed to spin out of focus. Ananya and Isha's physical confrontation reached a fever pitch, their breathing ragged and erratic. The intensity of their struggle overwhelmed them, and suddenly, everything went black. The room, once filled with shouts and violence, fell into a suffocating silence.

When Isha woke up on the floor the next morning, disoriented and groggy, her mind raced to piece together what had happened. She noticed Ananya lying on the bed, seemingly asleep. Panic gripped her as she recalled their fight, and she rushed out of the room to find Bharat.

"Bharat!" she gasped, finding him in the hallway. "Something happened last night... Ananya and I argued, and she hit me, and I pushed her. I—I don't know what happened after that!"

Bharat's heart sank. Realizing that Ananya might have discovered the truth about him and Isha, he hurried to the room. "Ananya," he called softly, approaching her. But when she didn't respond, dread washed over him. He tried shaking her awake, but her body was cold and unresponsive.

"Ananya!" Bharat's voice was choked with fear. "No... no, please wake up!" But it was too late—Ananya was gone.

Shock spread through the group like a chilling wave as they gathered in the dimly lit room, struggling to piece together the chaos of the night. The once lively atmosphere was now replaced with an eerie stillness, punctuated only by the hushed murmurs of concern and disbelief.

Isha stood apart from the group, her face ashen and her body trembling uncontrollably. Her eyes were wide with a mixture of fear and remorse. "I swear, I didn't mean to... I don't know what happened after I pushed her," she stammered, her voice thick with guilt. Her hands shook as she tried to make sense of the violent outburst. "I just lost control... I didn't intend for any of this."

The friends exchanged uneasy glances, their initial anger now tangled with confusion and concern. The argument had erupted into something far beyond their expectations, and now, the gravity of the situation was settling heavily on their shoulders.

Their attention shifted sharply to Bharat, who was frantically scrolling through Ananya's phone. His face grew increasingly pale as he absorbed the contents of her Instagram feed. Pings and notifications kept appearing, each one a stark reminder of a disturbing revelation. A video—an intimate moment between Bharat and Ananya—had been leaked and was now being viewed by countless strangers.

Bharat's hands trembled as he gripped the phone tightly, his expression a mixture of horror and despair. "I swear, I didn't share this with anyone," he pleaded, his voice desperate and strained. "I took the video, but it was only for us. It's always been in my phone. I didn't... I would never do this!"

His words hung in the air, heavy with the weight of his distress. The room fell into a tense silence as the reality of the situation sank in. The leaked video not only invaded their privacy but also exposed them to public scrutiny and judgment. The emotional and psychological impact of the breach was overwhelming.

Ananya's friends looked at each other, their expressions a blend of disbelief and sympathy. They were grappling with the realization that the video's leak was not just a violation of trust but a devastating breach of personal boundaries. The implications of the leaked content were far-reaching, affecting not just Ananya and Bharat but the entire group's dynamic.

As Bharat's voice broke under the strain of his emotions, he tried to explain further. "I don't know how this happened. I never wanted anyone else to see it. I kept it private... it was meant to be a personal moment between us."

The group's anger now turned inward, mingled with frustration over the breach of trust and the tangled web of emotions that had led to this moment. They felt the sting of betrayal, not just from the leaked video but from the night's violent confrontation. Each friend was left to confront their own feelings of guilt, shame, and helplessness as they faced the aftermath of their tumultuous evening.

The silence in the room was deafening as they struggled to come to terms with the reality of their situation. The bonds between them, once unbreakable, were now tested by the raw intensity of their emotions and the painful consequences of their actions.

The room fell silent, the weight of the situation crashing down on them. Ananya was dead, and the video leak pointed fingers at Bharat, but the truth was tangled in a web of secrets and misunderstandings. The friends, now overwhelmed by grief, shock, and fear, sat in different corners of the house, each lost in their own thoughts. Their minds raced with the same haunting question—what were they going to do?

Chapter 3: Whispers from the Void

The air was thick with tension and despair, the reality of Ananya's death weighing heavily on everyone. The room was shrouded in a suffocating silence, each person lost in their thoughts, consumed by guilt, confusion, and fear. The dim lighting only added to the sense of dread, casting long shadows that seemed to mirror their inner turmoil. The friends sat scattered around the room, their expressions a mix of sorrow and apprehension.

Chandra was the first to break the silence. He stood by the window, his gaze fixed on the distant city lights, as though searching for answers in the darkness. His voice, when he spoke, was calm yet resolute, a stark contrast to the storm brewing inside him. "We can't let this destroy all of us," he said, his tone steady but carrying an edge of urgency. "No one else needs to suffer more than we already have. We need to close this chapter and move on."

The group exchanged uneasy glances, their faces reflecting the same sense of dread and helplessness. The weight of Chandra's words hung in the air, a heavy reminder of the reality they were trying to escape. There was a moment of uncomfortable silence as they absorbed the gravity of the situation, the silence punctuated only by the occasional, nervous cough or the shuffling of feet.

Chandra took a deep breath, his eyes scanning the room. His gaze lingered on each person, searching for a sign of agreement. "I'll take care of everything," he said, his voice taking on a more authoritative tone. "We'll tell the police that Ananya took sleeping pills after discovering the leaked video.

That she couldn't handle the shame and took her own life.
The video only shows Ananya's face, not Bharat's. We don't
have to worry about implicating anyone else."

There was a heavy pause as the friends absorbed Chandra's
plan. Their faces reflected a mix of fear, doubt, and reluctant
acceptance. The idea of facing the truth, of letting the world
know what had truly happened, was too horrifying to
contemplate. The thought of their lives unravelling before
their eyes was almost more than they could bear. The
alternative—allowing the truth to come out—was far too
terrifying, and the prospect of their own ruin was a potent
deterrent.

One by one, they nodded in reluctant agreement. The
decision was made not out of conviction but out of necessity.
The group was united by their fear and the overwhelming
desire to protect themselves from the looming consequences.
They knew that sticking to the story Chandra had crafted was
their only option for escaping the nightmare they had created.

Chandra's gaze softened slightly as he took in their
agreement. "We'll need to be consistent with our story.
Remember, Ananya was alone when she took the pills. We
were all in different rooms, and no one saw anything
unusual."

The friends nodded again, their faces now showing a mix of
resignation and determination. They were all too aware of the
stakes, the price they might pay if they faltered. The silence
that followed was a heavy one, filled with unspoken fears and
the weight of their decision.

As they prepared to face the police and present their carefully crafted story, a sense of finality settled over them. The bonds they once shared were now strained, their friendship fractured by the dark secret they were concealing. The reality of their actions began to sink in, casting a long shadow over their futures. Yet, for now, they could do nothing but stick to the story they had agreed upon and hope that their deception would remain hidden in the shadows of their lives.

When the police arrived, the group prepared for the inevitable questioning, each member bracing themselves to present a consistent story. The air was thick with tension as they recounted their versions of the events leading up to Ananya's death.

Rakesh was the first to speak, his voice steady despite the anxiety that simmered beneath his composed exterior. "I was chatting with my sister that night. After that, we all moved to the terrace to drink. We were just having fun, and then we went to our rooms to sleep. We discovered Ananya in the morning."

Chandra, maintaining a calm demeanour, nodded in agreement. "After the terrace, the girls went to their room, and the rest of us went to ours. We found her in the morning."

Bharat, his face a mask of concern, added, "We had a cigarette and talked for a while before heading to bed. In the morning, we found Ananya."

Isha, trying to keep her voice steady, said, "I noticed Ananya seemed upset, but I thought she was just tired. I went to bed early, and when I woke up, she was… like this."

The officers took their statements, their faces impassive but scrutinizing. After gathering the initial information, they decided it was necessary to examine Ananya's body more thoroughly. They arranged for a post-mortem to be conducted to determine the cause of death and to ensure there were no signs of foul play.

The friends watched anxiously as the police prepared to transport Ananya's body to the morgue. Chandra had anticipated this step and had already arranged for a discreet bribe to ensure the process went smoothly. He slipped an envelope to one of the officers involved in the post-mortem arrangement, emphasizing the need for a swift and unobtrusive examination.

Hours later, the police returned with the report from the post-mortem. The official cause of death was ruled as an overdose of sleeping pills, consistent with the narrative Chandra had crafted. The report stated that Ananya had likely taken the pills in a moment of distress over the leaked video, confirming the story they had presented to the authorities.

With the cause of death officially recorded and the case marked as a suicide, the police closed the investigation. The friends were left with a fragile sense of relief, knowing that their story had held up under scrutiny. However, the truth of what had happened lingered like a dark cloud over them.

The resort, once a place of camaraderie and joy, now felt like a prison of guilt and fear. Each friend struggled with their own burden, knowing that while the case was closed, the repercussions of their actions would haunt them for a long time to come. The bond they once shared had been shattered, replaced by a heavy silence and the looming dread of what the future might bring

After leaving the resort, Bharat was a shadow of his former self. The carefree, adventurous spirit that once defined him had been replaced by a constant, gnawing anxiety. The memory of what he had done to Ananya and the tangled mess that followed plagued his thoughts. He locked himself in his room, avoiding everyone, and spent the entire day replaying the events in his mind, over and over again.

Guilt weighed heavily on Bharat, suffocating any sense of normalcy. Every time he closed his eyes, he saw Ananya's face—her eyes filled with betrayal, her lifeless body lying there. He couldn't escape the thoughts, no matter how hard he tried. Sleep evaded him, and by the time night fell, he was a wreck, exhausted yet wide awake. The weight of his actions pressed down on him, making it hard to breathe, to think, to live.

Rakesh, too, was plagued by guilt, though his was tinged with a sense of helplessness. As a horror enthusiast, he was familiar with tales of supernatural retribution, but facing it in reality was something entirely different. The dread of what had happened consumed him, turning his fascination into a source of fear. He couldn't shake the images of Ananya's final moments from his mind, and the fear that their actions might have triggered something beyond their control gnawed at him. The once-familiar comfort of horror movies now felt like a cruel reminder of their own dark reality.

Isha struggled with a mix of regret and self-loathing. The anger and jealousy she had felt seemed trivial compared to the magnitude of what had occurred. She replayed the argument with Ananya over and over, wishing she could turn back time and undo the moment of violence. Each time she tried to focus on her daily tasks, the image of Ananya's face haunted her, a constant reminder of her part in the tragedy. The guilt was overwhelming, and she felt a profound sense of isolation, as if she were trapped in a nightmare she couldn't escape.

It was around 3:00 AM when it happened. Bharat lay in his bed, the weight of his guilt pressing down on him, his eyes fixed on the darkened ceiling. The room was cloaked in shadows, the only light coming from the faint glow of the street lamps filtering through the curtains. The silence of the night was deep and oppressive, punctuated only by the occasional creak of the house settling.

As he stared into the darkness, trying to quiet the tumultuous thoughts racing through his mind, he suddenly heard it—a whisper, soft and haunting, yet unmistakable. The sound seemed to emanate from the very air around him, a chilling murmur that seemed to wrap itself around his senses.

"Bharat…"

The voice was eerily familiar, sending a shiver down his spine. It was Ananya's voice, or at least, it sounded like her. The whisper was so clear, so intimate, that it felt as if she were standing right beside him, speaking directly into his ear. Bharat's heart skipped a beat, and he froze, his breath catching in his throat.

His mind raced to make sense of the sound. He sat up abruptly, his eyes scanning the room in frantic search of the source. The shadows on the walls seemed to twist and writhe, and the once-familiar room now felt alien and foreboding. His pulse quickened, and a cold sweat broke out on his forehead. He felt a paralyzing fear, the kind that grips you when you realize you are alone in the dark, with something unseen and inexplicable.

A chilling sense of being watched crept over Bharat, making him feel as if he wasn't alone in the room. His mind raced with unsettling thoughts—what if some unseen force suddenly grabbed his legs and pulled him into the darkness? The dark corners of the room only intensified his fear, as if they were hiding something sinister. He tried desperately to steady his subconscious, battling the rising panic that threatened to consume him.

"Bharat…" The whisper came again, more insistent this time, as if calling out from the depths of a darkened abyss. The voice seemed to float through the room, weaving in and out of the silence, growing ever closer. Bharat's terror intensified; he could feel the presence more acutely now, as if it were encroaching on his very being.

He scrambled out of bed, his movements frantic and clumsy. His hands trembled as he reached for the light switch, desperate to banish the darkness and the haunting voice that seemed to linger just out of sight. The light flickered on, casting a harsh, sterile glow over the room. The familiar surroundings now felt cold and unwelcoming, the shadows receding but leaving behind a lingering sense of dread.

Bharat's gaze darted around the room, searching for any sign of an intruder or a rational explanation for the sound. The room was empty, the only evidence of his disturbance the overturned books and the dishevelled state of his bed. The whispering had stopped, leaving him in a silence that was now more oppressive than before.

He sank back onto the bed, his heart still racing. The fear that had gripped him now morphed into a cold, gnawing anxiety. Was he losing his mind? Was the guilt and stress of the past few days driving him to hallucinate? Or was there something more sinister at play?

As the hours stretched on and the night deepened, Bharat lay awake, unable to escape the haunting whisper and the suffocating sense of dread. The darkness outside seemed to press in on him, and the whispers in his mind grew louder with each passing moment. He knew one thing for certain— whatever this was, it was far from over.

 Bharat, shaken by the eerie whispers that haunted him throughout the night, knew he couldn't face this alone. Early the next morning, he went to Rakesh's place, his mind a whirlwind of fear and confusion. As he explained everything that had happened—the whispering voice, the sense of being watched, the overwhelming dread—Rakesh listened intently, his expression growing more serious with each word.

Rakesh had always been fascinated by the supernatural, and though he didn't voice it out loud, he was certain this was Ananya's ghost. There was no other explanation that made sense. But he didn't want to scare Bharat even more, so he kept his suspicions to himself.

"Bharat, listen," Rakesh said calmly, trying to ease his friend's anxiety. "There's no need to panic. Let's start by bringing some positive energy into your room. Light a diya and place it near a photo of Maa Durga. Her presence will protect you, and the light will drive away any negative forces. Try to sleep peacefully tonight, and let's see if things settle down."

Bharat nodded, desperate for any solution that might give him some peace. He returned home and followed Rakesh's advice, lighting the diya and placing it beside a framed picture of Maa Durga on his nightstand. The small flame flickered gently, casting a warm glow around the room. For the first time in days, Bharat felt a tiny flicker of hope that maybe, just maybe, things would get better.

But as the day went on, that hope was quickly shattered.

When Bharat returned to his room later that afternoon, he was met with a horrifying sight. The room was in complete disarray—books and clothes were strewn across the floor, his bed was upturned, and the diya, which had been burning steadily, was now extinguished. His heart raced as he took in the chaos. Something—or someone—had torn the room apart.

Panicking, Bharat called out to his mother, asking if she knew what had happened. But her response only deepened his fear.

"I don't know, Bharat," she said, her voice tinged with concern. "I didn't hear anything, and I haven't been in your room all day."

As Bharat surveyed the chaos in his room, his gaze fell upon a disturbing detail: a framed photo of the five friends, which had been hanging on the wall, was now shattered on the floor. The glass was broken into sharp, jagged pieces, and the picture itself was crumpled and torn. The sight sent a cold shiver down his spine, and a sense of foreboding washed over him.

"I'll take care of this, Mom," he said, trying to keep his voice steady. "Don't worry about it."

He knelt beside the wreckage, carefully picking up the photo. The faces of his friends were obscured by the broken glass and the torn edges, but Bharat could still make out the familiar features. It was as if the image had been violently torn apart, reflecting the turmoil and destruction that had recently unfolded.

His heart raced as he noticed something else—scratches on the frame and small, smeared handprints on the wall where the picture had been. They seemed to be smeared with something dark, almost like blood. Bharat's breath quickened, and he realized with a jolt that the handprints were not his own. The sense of dread that had been lurking in the back of his mind now surged forward, overwhelming him with a chilling certainty: Ananya's ghost was not just a figment of his imagination.

He stood up, his eyes scanning the room for more signs of disturbance. In the corner, he spotted a few books scattered across the floor, their pages torn. A closer look revealed that one of the books had a message scrawled across its open pages. The handwriting was jagged and erratic:

"You can't escape what you've done. The debt will be paid. All must suffer."

Bharat's pulse raced as he read the message, the implication clear. Ananya's spirit was angry, and it seemed to be preparing to exact revenge on everyone involved. The words felt like a direct threat, and Bharat understood that he, along with the others, was in grave danger.

He turned to the bedside table and noticed that his phone, which had been on silent, was now buzzing incessantly. When he picked it up, he saw a series of unsettling notifications. The screen was filled with messages from an unknown number, each one containing cryptic, threatening phrases:

"Guilt will consume you."

"One by one, you will pay."

"The truth will surface in blood."

A feeling of terror gripped him. The ghost's vendetta was taking shape, and the message was clear: Ananya intended to make each of them face the consequences of their actions. Bharat knew that he had to act quickly.

He took a deep breath, forcing himself to stay calm despite the panic rising within him. He needed to warn the others, to prepare them for the threat that was looming over them. There was no time to waste.

As he prepared to leave the house, he glanced back at the mess in his room. The disarray, the shattered photo, and the threatening messages all served as grim reminders that Ananya's vengeance was imminent. With a final, troubled look at the scene of chaos, Bharat rushed out of the house, determined to reach Rakesh, Isha, and Chandra before it was too late.They needed to know what had happened over the last two days, and they needed to figure out what they were dealing with—before it was too late.

Chapter 4: The Shattered veil

The room was thick with tension as Bharat recounted the terrifying events of the past two days. His voice quivered with fear as he described the whispers in Ananya's voice, the mess in his room, and the shattered photo of their group.

Everyone sat in stunned silence, the weight of Bharat's words pressing down on them. Isha, her arms tightly clasped around herself, struggled to control her breathing. Rakesh's eyes were wide with dawning realization, the gravity of their situation sinking in. Only Chandra seemed to hold onto a semblance of disbelief, though fear shadowed his gaze.

"We have to face it," Rakesh finally broke the silence, his voice laced with grim determination. "Ananya's spirit won't rest until it resolves whatever unfinished business she has. The longer she remains, the angrier she'll become. What she once was, is gone—now she's driven solely by vengeance."

From what I've read, spirits with unfinished business need to be faced head-on. Avoiding her or hiding from her will only make things worse."

Isha shivered, her thoughts racing as she tried to grasp the enormity of the situation. "What do we do? How can we stop this?"

Rakesh hesitated before speaking again. "There's a way, but it's not simple. According to an ancient text I read, a ghost can only be captured when its ties to this world are severed. But to confront Ananya, we need the help of someone who knows how to deal with spirits...someone who practices black magic."

"Who?" Bharat's voice was barely above a whisper.

"There's an old caveman who lives on the outskirts of the city. He's rumored to deal with these kinds of things, but only on a full moon," Rakesh explained, glancing nervously at the others. "And the next full moon is in three days."

 "Three days?" Isha's voice was filled with panic. "How do we survive until then? I can't live alone, not with this…thing haunting us."

Chandra, who had been quiet until now, finally spoke up, his voice steady. "Then we stay together. We don't leave each other's sight. If Ananya's spirit wants something, we can figure out what it is together. We'll stay strong."

Isha's voice trembled with fear. "So, we're supposed to face a vengeful spirit?

"Facing her might be our only option." Chandra said.

The others nodded, their fear tempered by Chandra's resolve. The reality of their situation was undeniable, and they had little choice but to confront the ghost. They agreed to stay together and face Ananya's spirit, hoping that their collective effort would be enough to keep them safe.

"We need to stick together and face whatever comes," Bharat said, his voice steadying as he spoke. "We can't afford to be divided or scared. We have to be brave and confront this head-on."

Rakesh, though still anxious, nodded in agreement. "Yes, we need to confront her and find out the ways to untie her bond with this real world. It's our only chance to end this."

As the group prepared to face the haunting presence of Ananya, they knew they were stepping into a dangerous and uncertain situation. The days leading up to the full moon would be fraught with tension and fear, but they had resolved to confront the ghost and seek a resolution.

Deep down, they all understood that facing Ananya's spirit was their only option. They had no other choice but to confront their fears, and hope that their unity and bravery would be enough to resolve the restless spirit's torment.

The three days ahead appeared like an eternity, each one a test of their sanity and survival. Ananya's spirit wasn't just a ghost—it was a reminder of the secrets they kept, the guilt they bore, and the fear that they might not all make it through alive.

The group sought out the caveman known for dealing with supernatural phenomena. Chandra booked a farmhouse on the outskirts of the city, near to caves ,hoping it would offer the solutions they desperately needed.

Upon arrival, they explained everything: Ananya's death, Bharat's eerie experiences, and their fears of the vengeful spirit. The caveman, an elderly figure with a deep, knowing gaze, listened intently. After a thoughtful pause, he asked, "Is that everything that happened?" When everyone nodded quietly in agreement, he offered his guidance.

"To deal with a spirit like hers," the caveman said in a gravelly voice, "you must sever the connections it has to the world of the living. You will need several items: lemon with three natural dots on it, red chilies soaked in the blood of a living being, and anything that belonged to Ananya—her dress, her nails, or her hair. Gather these items by the full moon night."

the group decided to spend the night at the farmhouse to prepare for the daunting task ahead. They needed rest and to be together, facing the night as a united front. The farmhouse, situated on the outskirts of the city, seemed to offer a temporary respite from the horrors that had plagued them.

As night fell, the farmhouse was cloaked in an eerie stillness. The group tried to settle down, each person battling their own fears and uncertainties. Exhausted but unable to fully relax, they retreated to their separate rooms, hoping that sleep would come despite the tension.

Rakesh, unable to sleep, decided to get some water from the kitchen. He tiptoed downstairs, trying to keep his mind occupied with mundane thoughts. Opening the fridge, he poured himself a glass of water, trying to calm his racing thoughts. The kitchen was dark, and the only sounds were the hum of the refrigerator and the distant creak of the farmhouse settling.

As he turned to head back to his room, Rakesh noticed a strange, faintly glowing object on the floor near the kitchen counter. It was partially obscured by the darkness, but something about it caught his eye. His heart raced as he moved closer, trying to make out what it was. The object seemed to be a broken piece of glass, but it was unusual and unsettling.

Suddenly, a sharp, grating sound pierced the silence—a cat's eerie yowl from outside, cutting through the night. The sound was sudden and jarring, making Rakesh jump. He stumbled backward, his heart pounding with sudden fear. The shadows in the kitchen seemed to twist and contort, adding to his disorientation.

Uncontrollably, Rakesh grabbed a knife from the counter, his hands shook, an overwhelming sense of dread washed over him. As if possessed by a malevolent force, he began to make several shallow cuts on his hand. The blade sliced through flesh with a disturbing precision, and blood dripped onto the floor in a chilling pattern.

As the blood pooled and spread out, it formed an eerie and symbolic shape—a clear message: **"Revolt is mine."** The crimson streaks on the floor seemed to spell out this warning in a haunting display with a weird smiley shape, urging the group to confront their fears and the spirit's demands. The pattern was both a chilling reminder and a direct challenge from Ananya's ghost.

The disturbing sight and the sound of his own ragged breathing broke through the haze of panic. The blood on the floor took on an almost sentient quality, a stark reminder of the consequences of their actions. The warning seemed to pulse with a dark energy, demanding that they face the spirit's vengeance and the guilt that weighed heavily on their souls.

Hearing the commotion and the unsettling sound of Rakesh's erratic movements, the others rushed downstairs. Chandra, Bharat, and Isha found Rakesh standing in the dim kitchen, his hands bloodied and his expression vacant with shock. The sight of the blood on the floor was chilling, and the message it seemed to convey left them stunned.

"What's going on?" Chandra's voice was tight with concern as he approached Rakesh, trying to assess the situation.

Bharat and Isha stood back, their faces pale as they took in the scene. Bharat's eyes were wide with alarm, while Isha's hands shook as she reached out to help Rakesh.

Rakesh, still in a daze, looked at the bloodstains with a mixture of fear and confusion. "I couldn't control myself..." he muttered, his voice trembling. "It was like something else was... controlling me."

Chandra quickly took action, grabbing a towel and applying pressure to Rakesh's wounds. Bharat helped to clean up the blood, while Isha tried to comfort Rakesh, who was still in shock.

"We need to get this cleaned up and take care of Rakesh," Chandra said firmly. "But we also need to talk about this. Whatever is happening here, it's getting worse."

The group managed to clean up the mess and tend to Rakesh's wounds. The blood on the floor remained as a stark reminder of the mounting tension and fear, a visual representation of the spirit's influence and the dire situation they faced.

As dawn approached, the group gathered in the living room, their exhaustion evident. Isha and Rakesh, still reeling from the night's events, tried to offer support.

The disturbing events of the previous night had only heightened their sense of urgency. They knew they had no choice but to face Ananya's spirit directly and gather the items necessary for the ritual to sever her ties to the world. Despite their fears, they resolved to see the task through, hoping that their combined efforts would be enough to put an end to the haunting and resolve the restless spirit's torment.

Chandra and Bharat took on the task of gathering the items which cavemen asked, while Isha and Rakesh stayed at the farmhouse. The journey to acquire the components was fraught with tension. Bharat tried to distract himself from the creeping dread by engaging in casual conversation with Chandra, but the unease lingered.

As they drove, Bharat's attention was suddenly drawn to the road. He slammed on the brakes as he thought he saw Ananya standing in the middle of the road. The car screeched to a halt almost about to crash, and Chandra's heart pounded with sudden alarm.

"What's wrong?" Chandra asked, his voice tight with concern.

"I thought I saw Ananya," Bharat replied, his face pale and eyes wide. "But she was gone when I looked again."

Chandra scanned the road but saw nothing out of the ordinary. "Are you sure? Maybe it was just your mind playing tricks on you."

Bharat nodded, though his mind remained haunted by the fleeting vision. As Chandra resumed driving, Bharat stared out the window, lost in memories of Ananya. The streets blurred together, each landmark evoking past moments shared with her. His thoughts were tangled in guilt, sadness, and the haunting realization of his loss.

Back at the farmhouse, Isha and Rakesh anxiously awaited Chandra and Bharat's return. The night was thick with tension as they prepared for what lay ahead. Rakesh, his anxiety mounting, chanted the Hanuman Chalisa to stave off the encroaching fear. Isha, equally unsettled, couldn't help but probe further.

"Rakesh," Isha began, her voice trembling slightly, "do you remember anything about the night Ananya died? Do you know what really happened?"

Rakesh shook his head, his face ashen. "No, I don't remember much. Everything's a blur."

Suddenly, a loud, jarring banging on the door shattered the silence, causing both Isha and Rakesh to jump. Their hearts pounded as they gripped each other's hands for support.

"What was that?" Isha whispered, her voice trembling.

"I don't know," Rakesh replied, his fear evident. "Let's check it out."

With a mix of dread and determination, Rakesh approached the door, with Isha standing hesitantly behind him. He slowly opened it, and to his astonishment, Isha stood outside carrying medicines, her face ashen and eyes wide with confusion seeing Rakesh's Expression. As he turned back, the room was empty, and the oppressive silence deepened their unease.

"What?" Rakesh stammered, his eyes darting between the Isha in front of him and the empty room behind him. "Who was that…?"

"I don't understand," Isha said, her voice shaky.

Rakesh, still reeling from the shock, looked at Isha in disbelief. The ghostly apparition had been a disturbing mimicry of her, and the realization left him trembling.

"I swear I saw someone who looked just like you," Rakesh said, trying to steady his voice. "But now... it's gone."

"What, I went to get some medicine for your cuts. How could there be another me?"Isha said in low tone.

Isha, equally disoriented, tried to comfort Rakesh, but the fear between them was palpable.

The Thunderous noises from above, deepened their growing dread, adding a new layer of terror to their already harrowing situation. As they tried to make sense of what had happened, a cold silence settled over them, a haunting reminder that they were not alone in the farmhouse.

They decided to check the unsettling noise. Isha, her face on a mask of worry, headed towards another room to check if there was any sign of disturbance or an explanation for the mysterious figure. She moved cautiously, her heart pounding in her chest, as she peered into the dimly lit hallway. The house felt unnaturally cold, and the shadows seemed to stretch and bend in unnatural ways.

Suddenly, she caught a glimpse of movement out of the corner of her eye. A figure stood at the far end of the hallway, its form barely visible in the darkness. Isha squinted, trying to make out who it was. As she stepped closer, the figure came into focus, and her blood ran cold—it was Ananya, or rather, something that looked like her.

Before Isha could react, the ghostly figure lunged at her. Ananya's ghost grabbed her with inhuman strength, slamming her against the wall. Isha gasped in pain, her eyes wide with terror as she looked into the vengeful eyes of her once-friend.

"You took everything from me," the ghost hissed, her voice dripping with venom. "Now it's my turn."

Isha struggled to break free, but the ghost held her firm, lifting her off the ground as if she weighed nothing. "My trust, my friendship—everything I held dear—you destroyed it well! You never understood, did you? The pain of knowing that those closest to me, were the ones who betrayed me."

Ananya's ghost tightened her grip on Isha, lifting her higher against the wall. Her eyes burned with fury as she continued, her voice rising with each word. "I was nothing to you! A pawn in your game, something to be discarded when I was no longer useful. You laughed, you smiled, but behind my back, you plotted against me. Did you think I wouldn't find out?"

Isha's eyes filled with tears as the ghost's words cut into her like a blade. The raw pain and betrayal in Ananya's voice were impossible to ignore.

"I trusted you!" the ghost screamed, her voice cracking with the intensity of her anger. "I believed you were my friend, but you were just waiting for me to fall, to take everything I had. You wanted what I had, but you couldn't have it, could you? So you destroyed it instead!"

The ghost's face twisted into a mask of rage and sorrow as she yanked Isha by the hair, dragging her down the stairs with terrifying strength. "You left me with nothing but pain, and now, I'll make sure you feel every ounce of it. You'll know what it's like to have everything ripped away, to be alone, afraid, and broken!"

Reaching the bottom of the stairs, Ananya's ghost materialized a sharp axe from thin air. With a cold, deliberate motion, she raised the weapon, her eyes locked on Isha, ready to exact her deadly revenge. Isha, fuelled by a desperate will to survive, twisted her body just in time, causing the axe to miss its mark by inches.

In a panic, Isha scrambled to her feet, bolting towards another room. She dashed inside, her breaths ragged and frantic, and hid in the corner, pressing herself against the wall. She held her breath, praying that the ghost wouldn't find her, as the sound of heavy footsteps echoed in the hallway outside.

Whereas Rakesh, trembling but determined, stayed behind to secure the area. He moved cautiously towards the window, the room around him feeling colder than before. As he drew the curtains closed, he heard a strange, almost imperceptible rustling sound, like a whisper carried by the wind. The shifting air seemed to wrap around him, carrying with it faint, eerie murmurs that sent a shiver down his spine. The whispers were indistinct, like fragments of a conversation he couldn't quite grasp, but their presence was undeniably unsettling.

Rakesh's heart raced as he strained to hear through the unsettling silence that followed. He called out for Isha, his voice wavering, "Isha? Are you there?"

Isha, pressed tightly into the corner of the dimly lit room, couldn't respond. Ananya's ghostly presence loomed just inches away, her cold, hollow eyes locked onto Isha's trembling form. Isha's heart pounded in her chest, each beat echoing in her ears as she tried to hold back her tears, her breath shallow and ragged.

She wanted to scream, to call out to Rakesh for help, but the icy grip of fear held her captive. The ghost's malevolent aura was suffocating, and Isha could feel the cold seeping into her bones. She clamped a hand over her mouth, stifling the sobs that threatened to escape, knowing that any sound could draw the ghost's wrath.

As Rakesh's voice echoed faintly through the walls, Isha remained frozen in place, desperately willing herself to be invisible, hoping that the ghost would eventually turn away. But Ananya's ghostly form lingered, her presence a chilling reminder that the nightmare was far from over.

The only response to Rakesh was the oppressive silence that settled heavily over the room. The quiet was deafening, each second stretching into an eternity. Rakesh's anxiety mounted, his mind racing through dark thoughts as he peered into the dimly lit room.

He took a deep breath, trying to steady himself, but the silence was unnerving. The rustling whispers seemed to grow louder, though still indistinguishable. His gaze darted nervously around the room, searching for any sign of movement or explanation.

"Isha!" he called again, his voice cracking with fear. Still, no reply came. The room remained eerily still, and the whispers ceased as suddenly as they had started.

Rakesh's pulse quickened as he turned his attention back to the window, his hands shaking. The realization that he was alone in the room, with no sign of Isha, heightened his sense of dread. The darkness outside seemed to press in closer, intensifying the feeling of isolation and fear.

A sense of foreboding filled the air, and Rakesh felt as if he was being watched, the hairs on the back of his neck standing on end. He fought against the rising panic, trying to piece together what was happening. Every creak and groan of the farmhouse seemed amplified, each sound a potential threat in the quiet night.

As he hesitated, the fear of being alone with whatever was causing the disturbances overwhelmed him. He called out for Isha one more time, his voice barely a whisper, "Isha, please come back."

But the silence remained, a chilling reminder that something was very wrong, and Rakesh's growing anxiety left him paralyzed with fear, unsure of what to do next.

Suddenly, Rakesh saw a shadowy figure standing ominously before him. His blood ran cold as he realized the figure was not Isha but something far more sinister. Panic overtook him, and he stumbled downstairs, desperate to escape whatever horror awaited him. But as he reached the bottom, the sight that met his eyes was nightmarish: Isha, headless and lifeless, slumped on the couch, clutching Rakesh's phone. On the screen was the leaked video of Ananya, playing on a loop.

Rakesh's blood ran cold as the horrifying reality sank in. Ananya's ghost had exacted its vengeance, and Isha had become its victim. Overwhelmed with terror and guilt, Rakesh collapsed into a corner, paralyzed by fear. His mind raced, recalling how he had accessed Bharat's phone when he borrowed to chat with his sister at the resort, viewed the videos, and forwarded them to his own device. The video had likely leaked due to vulnerabilities in his phone, caused by the loan applications he had installed, exposing him to hackers.

As he sat there, trembling and unable to move, he heard a faint, desperate voice calling his name. It was Isha, her voice filled with a mixture of confusion and terror. She came stumbling into the room, shouting his name, but Rakesh was too consumed by his own fear and the gruesome sight before him to register her presence.

"Isha...Isha, I'm so sorry," Rakesh muttered, his eyes fixed on the headless body on the couch.

Isha stopped in her tracks, her breath catching in her throat as she followed his gaze. Her eyes widened in horror as she saw her own lifeless body lying there, headless, the blood still pooling on the couch. A wave of disbelief washed over her as she reached up to touch her own head, only to find that the axe had indeed struck true. The memory of the ghostly encounter flooded back—how Ananya's spirit had lifted the axe and how she had tried to escape but failed.

A cold, eerie silence enveloped the room as the realization dawned on Isha. She was dead—murdered by the vengeful spirit of her former friend. The chilling truth sank in, and she let out a scream of pure anguish, a scream that seemed to echo endlessly in the oppressive stillness of the farmhouse.

But Rakesh couldn't hear her. To him, Isha's scream was nothing more than the faintest whisper of wind, lost in the cacophony of his own spiralling despair. He could only stare at the gruesome scene before him, haunted by the consequences of his actions, now realizing that there was no escape from the fate Ananya's ghost had decreed.

The enormity of his wrongdoing weighed heavily on Rakesh, pressing down on him like a suffocating weight. He had contributed to Ananya's death, and now her ghost's wrath was manifesting in terrifying and unimaginable ways. His fear intensified, and as he sat hunched in the corner, trying to fend off the rising panic, the walls of the farmhouse seemed to close in on him, making it harder to breathe.

As the night dragged on, Rakesh's terror became a living, breathing thing, gnawing at his sanity. The silence in the farmhouse was unbearable, broken only by the sound of his ragged breathing. He felt completely alone, abandoned to the horrors that surrounded him, until—finally—he heard the familiar voices of Bharat and Chandra echoing through the house.

Their arrival brought a fleeting glimmer of hope. Rakesh's heart pounded as he saw them approach, their faces etched with concern. It was as if they had arrived just in time to save him from the brink of madness. But the nightmare was far from over.

Upon seeing Isha's lifeless body on the couch, Chandra and Bharat were struck with horror. Chandra's face went pale as he processed the scene before him, the gravity of the situation hitting him like a ton of bricks. leaving him paralyzed with fear. Bharat's usual carefree demeanour was replaced by a mask of shock and disbelief. The air was thick with tension, and the reality of the situation weighed heavily on all of them.

Rakesh, trembling uncontrollably, recounted everything in a frantic, disjointed manner. He spoke of how the video might have leaked, how he had forwarded it to his own device, and how the vulnerabilities in his phone from the loan applications had likely exposed him to hackers. Each word was laced with guilt and dread, as he realized the role he had played in unleashing the horrors they were now facing.

The stress and fear were obvious as they all realized how dangerous their situation was. Chandra and Bharat looked at each other with concern, trying to stay calm. They knew they had to remain composed, but Rakesh was beyond help. The events of the night had left him unable to think clearly, his mind sinking into a dark place with no way out.

Bharat tried to calm him down, to convince him to stay with them, emphasizing the need for unity in the face of such overwhelming terror. But Rakesh was resolute, his guilt and fear pushing him to the edge. He needed to escape, to get away from the nightmare that had consumed him.

Desperate, Rakesh stumbled toward the door, barely registering Bharat's pleas to stay. He was fixated on one thing: escape. The moment he stepped outside, the cold air hit him like a slap in the face, jolting him back to the horrifying reality. As he looked around, the once-familiar surroundings now seemed distorted, twisted by the malevolent force that had taken over his life.

Just as he reached the edge of the woods, he turned back to see something that made his blood run cold. Standing before him was not Bharat or Chandra, but Isha's ghostly apparition, her eyes filled with sorrow and accusation. She stared at him with an intensity that pierced his very soul, and in that moment, Rakesh knew there was no escaping the consequences of his actions.

A scream of terror escaped his lips as he bolted into the woods, driven by a primal need to flee. The trees seemed to close in around him, the shadows stretching and twisting into nightmarish shapes. Every step he took felt like running through quicksand, the fear gripping him tighter with each passing moment. But no matter how fast he ran, he couldn't outrun the relentless fear that consumed him, nor could he escape the ghostly presence that seemed to follow him at every turn.

His mind was a whirlpool of confusion and terror, and reality began to blur. He heard Chandra and Bharat's voices again, calling out to him from somewhere deep within the woods. But were they really there, or was it just another cruel trick of his tormented mind? He couldn't tell anymore. He was lost, both in the woods and in his own spiralling fear.

As he stumbled through the dark forest, the echoes of his friends' voices grew louder, more urgent. "Rakesh, stop! Come back! We're here to help!" Bharat's voice rang out, filled with desperation.

Rakesh slowed down, his breath coming in ragged gasps as he tried to understand what was happening. He turned around, his vision blurring, and saw the shapes of Bharat and Chandra coming through the trees. For a moment, he felt a glimmer of hope.

But as they got closer, that hope vanished. The figures he thought were his friends turned into horrifying, twisted versions of themselves, their faces full of cruelty. It hit him hard—he had been tricked. The ghost had been playing with his mind, showing him fake safety to drag him further into fear.

Rakesh's scream echoed through the dark woods as he collapsed to the ground, consumed by the overwhelming terror that there was **no escape—not from the woods, not from the Ananya, and not from the crushing guilt that would haunt him for the rest of his days.**

Chapter 5 Echoes of Betrayal

As Chandra and Bharat were driving back through the dense woods, Bharat suddenly noticed something lying in the shadows near the driveway. He squinted through the darkness and realized it was a figure sprawled on the ground.

"Stop the car!" Bharat exclaimed, his voice tight with urgency.

Chandra hit the brakes, and they both rushed out to investigate. As they got closer, they recognized Rakesh lying motionless on the forest floor, his clothes dishevelled and his face pale.

"Rakesh!" Chandra shouted, shaking him awake.

Rakesh stirred, his eyes fluttering open. He looked at them with a mix of fear and exhaustion. "It's all real... the ghost... she... she's everywhere."

Without wasting any time, Chandra and Bharat helped Rakesh back to the car and drove him to the farmhouse. As they listened to his trembling voice recount the terrifying events—the ghostly apparition of Isha, her headless body on the couch, and his descent into fear—they felt a chill run down their spines. The reality of their situation weighed heavily on them; they had just one night left before the full moon, and they knew the danger was far from over.

Knowing they couldn't risk staying at the farmhouse any longer, the three friends made a unanimous decision. They drove straight to the remote chamber of small caves in the hills, where the cavemen resided, seeking refuge and help from the only ones who might understand what was happening.

The chamber was a foreboding place, surrounded by dense woods and bathed in an eerie glow under the waning moonlight. The cavemen, engaged in dark rituals, barely acknowledged their arrival. The cries of young girls, possessed by unseen forces, echoed through the air, sending shivers down their spines.

The cavemen explained that the full moon would bring powerful energies, intensifying the rituals they practiced. They offered the trio a small, isolated chamber for the night—a cold, dimly lit room with flickering candles casting unsettling shadows on the walls.

Chandra, Bharat, and Rakesh settled into the chamber, their hearts heavy with fear and uncertainty. As the night wore on, the realization that they were now part of something far beyond their understanding began to sink in. They had sought refuge here, but the horrors they faced might only be just beginning.

As they settled into the eerie chamber, the oppressive atmosphere seemed to thicken with every passing moment. The flickering candlelight cast unsettling shadows on the walls, and an unnatural chill permeated the air. Just when the silence seemed unbearable, a faint whisper echoed through the chamber, chilling Bharat to the bone.

"Bharat..." The voice was soft, almost tender, but it carried an unmistakable weight of sorrow and anger.

Bharat's heart skipped a beat. He looked at Chandra and Rakesh, but they seemed oblivious to the voice. The mounting tension was overwhelming, and the thought of Isha's gruesome death weighed heavily on him. Fearing that she might come for him, he knew he would be safer in the caves where Lord Kali was present. Desperate to escape whatever was coming, he decided to step outside, determined to save himself, even if it meant leaving Chandra and Rakesh behind.

The darkness outside was nearly impenetrable, with the dense trees casting long, twisted shadows under the faint light of the moon. Bharat ventured into the woods, heading straight for the inner caves. His steps were hesitant, and his breath came in shallow gasps. Every rustle of leaves and snap of twigs made his heart race. With a few more steps, he hoped he would reach safety.

Suddenly, a shadow darted past his right ear, so close that he felt a cold gust of air brush against his skin. Startled, Bharat stumbled backward, his fear escalating. Before he could regain his footing, an unseen force gripped him, lifting him off the ground with an unnatural strength. He was slammed against a tree, the bark digging into his back, as a choking pressure wrapped around his neck.

Panic surged through him as he clawed at his throat, trying to break free from the invisible grip. Then, a disembodied voice echoed through the trees, its tone filled with a haunting mix of sorrow and vengeance. "It was you who first killed me."

The voice was unmistakably Ananya's. Bharat's mind raced as he struggled to breathe, the weight of guilt crushing him as heavily as the unseen force around his neck. He wanted to shout, to apologize, but his voice was lost in the vice-like grip of the spirit.

Just as suddenly as it had begun, the pressure around his neck released, and Bharat collapsed to the ground, gasping for air. Desperate to escape the unseen terror, he scrambled to his feet and ran blindly through the woods, the shadows twisting and contorting around him.

As Bharat stumbled through the darkened woods, gasping for breath, the echoes of Ananya's voice reverberated in his mind, each syllable dripping with sorrow and accusation. The oppressive darkness seemed to close in around him, the twisted shadows dancing threateningly at the edges of his vision. His pulse pounded in his ears, drowning out all rational thought, leaving only raw fear in its wake.

Suddenly, out of the suffocating darkness, a figure emerged. Bharat halted in his tracks, his heart lurching in his chest. It was Isha. Her figure looked almost ghostly, illuminated by the soft light coming through the tangled branches above. Her face was a picture of concern, her eyes wide with worry. She rushed toward him, her voice soft and urgent.

"Bharat, it's me," she whispered, her tone soothing, laced with an undercurrent of desperation. "We need to get out of here. Now."

Relief flooded Bharat's senses at the sight of her, grounding him in the chaotic whirlwind of his emotions. "Isha… I thought I was—" His voice trembled, the words caught in his throat.

"I know," she cut him off gently, placing a hand on his cheek. The warmth of her touch was a stark contrast to the bone-chilling cold that had settled deep in his bones. "But you're safe now. We're safe."

Bharat's gaze searched hers, finding solace in the familiar tenderness of her expression. She stepped closer, her hand slipping from his cheek to trail softly down his arm, her fingers intertwining with his. The simple touch sent a wave of warmth through him, chasing away the remnants of fear that had held him captive.

Isha leaned in, her breath warm against his skin as she whispered, "We can get through this together. You're not alone."

In that moment, Bharat felt the overwhelming tension begin to ebb away, replaced by a deep, unspoken connection between them. The nightmarish reality of the woods seemed to fade into the background, leaving only the two of them in the stillness of the night. Her presence, her touch, became an anchor in the storm that had been raging within him.

Without thinking, he pulled her closer, his hands finding the curve of her waist. The desperation in him gave way to a longing for comfort, for an escape from the torment that had been haunting him. He captured her lips with his, the kiss slow and searching, as if trying to find solace in the warmth of her embrace.

Isha responded in kind, her arms wrapping around his neck, pulling him even closer. The kiss deepened, the intensity of the moment heightening as the fear and pain of the past seemed to melt away in the heat of their shared passion. Her fingers wove through his hair, tugging slightly, eliciting a low moan from him that vibrated through the night air.

But as the kiss continued, something shifted. The warmth of her lips grew cold, the tenderness turning into something far more sinister. Bharat's mind, clouded by the sudden surge of passion, didn't register the change at first. But then, as he opened his eyes slightly, he noticed the once-soft features of Isha's face had contorted into a twisted, mocking grin. Her eyes gleamed with a dark, malevolent light.

His heart pounded in his chest as he pulled back, the terror rushing back in full force. "Isha…?" His voice was barely a whisper, tinged with disbelief.

But it wasn't Isha standing before him anymore. The figure before him flickered and shifted, revealing Ananya's ghostly form. Her cold, vengeful eyes bore into his, the satisfaction of her deception written all over her face.

"You fell for it so easily," Ananya's voice hissed, the sound like nails on a chalkboard, sending chills down Bharat's spine.

Before he could react, Ananya's ghostly form lunged forward, her once-loving eyes now filled with pure malice. Her hands, cold as death itself, gripped his shoulders with inhuman strength, forcing him down to his knees.

Bharat struggled, but it was pointless. Ananya's ghost leaned in close, her voice a chilling whisper in his ear. "Is it a sin to be loyal, Bharat? Are you so blinded by your own desires that you can't see the truth?"

With a twisted smile, she produced a gleaming blade from the shadows, the metal catching the faint light of the moon as she brandished it before his eyes. Bharat's breath hitched in his throat as terror overwhelmed him, rendering him completely helpless in her grasp.

The blade cut across his lips first, the sharp pain making him scream, but his cries were silenced as blood filled his mouth. Ananya moved with cold precision, her actions almost robotic as she attacked him. She then cut down to his genitals, inflicting deep, unbearable pain unlike anything he'd ever felt.

Bharat's mind went into shock, his thoughts a blur of pain and regret as he saw Ananya with a fierce expression, her red eyes filled with tears of angry love. But Ananya wasn't finished; she dragged the blade across his throat and drove her sharp, flexed tongue into his spine, slicing through flesh and muscle. With a sickening finality, she ended his life.

As Bharat fell to the ground, blood pouring from his wounds, the final image seared into his mind was Ananya's twisted, sorrowful face. Her expression spoke of a cruel revenge fulfilled and a devastating act against the one she once loved. The world around him dimmed, his vision fading into darkness as life ebbed away, leaving only the cold, empty void behind. As his life ended, the crushing weight of guilt and sorrow overwhelmed him, leaving him to die with a heart full of regret.

Back at the chamber, Chandra and Rakesh anxiously called out for Bharat, who had disappeared without a word. The fear that had been growing all night now felt like a heavy, tangible presence pressing down on them. When Bharat didn't answer, Chandra and Rakesh decided they had no choice but to search for him.

As they ventured into the woods, Chandra's anxiety grew. The shadows of the forest seemed to move and shift ominously. They called out for Bharat, but the only response was the unsettling silence of the night.

Eventually, they found Bharat's belongings scattered and signs of his struggle only deepened their dread. The dense forest enveloped them in darkness, the only light coming from the occasional flicker of moonlight through the thick canopy. Chandra led the search, his eyes scanning the shadowy woods with urgency. Rakesh followed, his face pale and his thoughts clouded by dread.

Despite their efforts to call out for Bharat, the forest remained eerily silent, amplifying their growing anxiety. The silence was occasionally broken by the rustling of leaves and the distant calls of nocturnal creatures, but it offered little comfort.

Suddenly, Chandra and Rakesh stumbled upon a grim scene. Bharat's body lay sprawled on the forest floor, barely recognizable except by the belongings that marked him. Chandra's heart sank as he knelt beside the body, grappling with the grim reality of their situation.

As Chandra examined the body, Rakesh's face contorted with a mix of confusion and fear. A shadow of malevolence seemed to overtake him, and his eyes glazed over with a haunting emptiness.

Rakesh, now seemingly possessed by Ananya's vengeful spirit, turned toward Chandra with a cold, malicious grin. His voice, hollow and filled with dark energy, sent a chill through the air as he sneered, "You think I don't know what you've done?" With sudden, terrifying intensity, he lunged at Chandra, brandishing a sharp, narrow stick.

Chandra's eyes widened in shock and fear as the sharp edge of the stick came dangerously close to his eyes. Realizing the threat, he quickly grabbed Rakesh and pushed him away, shouting, "Rakesh, snap out of it! What are you doing? You almost killed me!"

The force of Chandra's push seemed to break the possession, and Rakesh collapsed to the ground, his expression clearing as he looked up at Chandra with a mix of confusion and horror. "Chandra… What happened? What did I do?"

Chandra, his heart racing, helped Rakesh to his feet. "We need to keep moving. We can't let this night consume us."

As Chandra and Rakesh made their way back to the cavemen's chamber, the oppressive atmosphere of the night weighed heavily upon them. Their recent encounter with the horrors of the forest had left them shaken, and the urgency to seek refuge among the cavemen was palpable. The night air was thick with an unsettling silence, broken only by the occasional rustle of leaves and the distant call of nocturnal creatures.

Their steps were heavy and weary as they navigated the moonlit woods, the shadows of the trees stretching long and eerie in the pale light. Chandra, determined but visibly anxious, led the way, his thoughts consumed by the peril they faced. Rakesh followed close behind, his mind still grappling with the horror of recent events.

As they approached the chamber, Chandra's anxiety was tinged with a sense of grim resolve. They had hoped for some respite, a chance to regroup and confront the malevolent forces that had disrupted their lives. However, the chamber's atmosphere offered no comfort.

Inside the chamber, Rakesh was overwhelmed by the sight of the cruel aftermath of their recent events. The memories of Isha and Bharat's deaths haunted him— Isha's headless body and Bharat's mangled form were deeply etched in his mind. Though their bodies were not physically present, they served as a constant reminder of the brutality and loss that had overtaken them.

Rakesh's heart ached with guilt and terror as he reflected on the horrors. Tears streamed down his face as he grappled with the weight of his responsibility. His voice trembled with anguish as he murmured, " Isha was beheaded for her betrayal, despite being an only trusted female friend. Bharat—Ananya's world and trust and everything, shattered her by cheating. I realize now that I crossed boundaries and failed to respect their trust and privacy. I was responsible in leaking the video that covered up her murder and tarnished her reputation even after her death. I am responsible for this."

Chandra, hearing Rakesh's frantic whispers, turned sharply. "Shut up, Rakesh," he said, his voice firm but filled with concern. "We're going to fight this."

But Rakesh's despair was too deep. "You don't understand," he pleaded. "She will kill me…… She will kill me."

The weight of Rakesh's despair became unbearable. In a moment of profound hopelessness, he ended his life by plunging from the edge of the deep valley near the cave. His remorse was almost tangible, driving him toward the edge. Standing at the brink, the whispers of his regrets were carried away by the wind, and with a final, anguished step, he disappeared into the void below,leaving Chandra in shock and deep mourning.

In the aftermath, Chandra stood in the chamber, the magnitude of their losses crashing down on him. The chamber, filled with the echoes of their grief and the oppressive silence of the night, became a haunting reminder of the darkness they faced. With only one night left to confront the malevolent forces and seek a way out of the abyss, Chandra's resolve hardened. The urgency of their quest for survival and redemption was now more critical than ever.

Desperate to save himself, Chandra reached the cavemen and implored them to perform the necessary rituals immediately, even though the full moon was still a day away. The cavemen, sensing the urgency in Chandra's voice and the terror in his eyes, agreed to begin the rites without delay.

Inside the chamber, the cavemen moved with a grim determination. They set up their ritual space with precision, arranging ancient symbols and laying out offerings. The air quickly filled with the heavy scent of burning herbs, and the dim light of flickering candles created a surreal, almost oppressive atmosphere. Chandra, his heart racing and his mind a whirl of grief and fear, watched anxiously as the cavemen chanted ancient mantras and performed the rites designed to appease Ananya's restless spirit.

The chamber seemed to close in on them as the rituals continued, the shadows cast by the candles dancing menacingly on the walls. Each chant and gesture by the cavemen was accompanied by an unsettling silence, broken only by the occasional crackle of the burning herbs and the distant howling of the wind outside. Chandra's nerves were frayed, his anxiety mounting with every passing minute. He clung to the hope that these rites would finally bring an end to the haunting that had claimed so many lives.

Suddenly, the calm was shattered. A gust of wind, unnatural and fierce, howled through the chamber, extinguishing several candles and plunging the room into darkness. The flames flickered wildly before dying out completely, and the room was swallowed by an oppressive blackness. Panic surged through Chandra as he fumbled for a light source, but the cavemen remained eerily calm, their chanting becoming more frantic and desperate.

In the sudden darkness, the temperature in the room plummeted, and a deep, bone-chilling cold settled over everything. The once-distant howling of the wind grew louder, now a cacophony of mournful cries that seemed to seep into the walls. Shadows seemed to twist and writhe as if alive, adding to the surreal, nightmarish atmosphere.

Chandra's heart pounded in his chest as he saw a shadowy figure move in the periphery of the room. He squinted, trying to make out its form, but it remained elusive, darting from one corner to another. The chanting of the cavemen grew increasingly erratic, their voices strained and desperate as they fought to maintain their focus amidst the chaos.

As Chandra's fear grew, he saw something that made his blood freeze: Ananya's ghostly figure appeared at the edge of the room, her eyes glowing with a vengeful light, her body covered in blood, and surrounded by fog. Her once-beautiful face was twisted with pain and anger. The shadowy figure seemed to shift and change, making it hard to see its true shape.

In a fit of terror, Chandra screamed, "What's happening? Why isn't it working?"

The cavemen shouted back, their voices barely audible over the howling wind. "The spirit's power is stronger than anticipated! The rituals must continue, but we must hold fast!"

Just then, the oppressive cold intensified, and a sudden force seemed to slam against the walls of the chamber, shaking it violently. The candles were relit by a gust of wind, but the flickering light only added to the disorienting effect. Chandra felt an unnatural presence closing in on him, its malevolent energy suffocating.

Desperate, he tried to assist the cavemen, but his efforts seemed futile against the overpowering force of Ananya's spirit. The chamber seemed to pulse with dark energy, and the walls seemed to groan under the strain of the spirit's rage.

As the night wore on, the tension in the chamber reached a fever pitch. The cavemen's chants became almost frenzied, their movements desperate as they struggled to maintain control. Chandra, overwhelmed by a mix of fear, guilt, and sorrow, clung to the hope that the rituals would ultimately be successful. Yet, moon cast its cold light over the landscape, the outcome remained shrouded in uncertainty, and the night continued its ominous course, with every moment adding to the palpable dread that gripped the chamber.

As the cavemen continued their rituals, the heavy atmosphere in the chamber seemed to move like it was alive. Shadows on the walls flickered wildly, and the room's temperature kept changing between freezing and sweltering. The ritual reached its peak as the cavemen, their voices hoarse from hours of chanting, performed the final rites with urgent intensity.

Suddenly, the chamber grew silent. The flickering candles, after enduring the intense energy of the ritual, now gave off a steady, calming light. The heavy feeling in the room lifted, replaced by an eerie calm. The shadows on the walls, which had once been twisted and threatening, now took on harmless shapes.

Chandra, soaked in sweat and shaking, took a cautious breath. The overwhelming fear that had filled the room began to fade, giving way to a strange, calm stillness. The cavemen, exhausted, started to relax. Their chanting had stopped, and they moved slowly, as if the air around them had become lighter.

The elder caveman, his expression a blend of relief and solemnity, approached Chandra. "The rituals are complete, and the spirit's rage has been subdued—at least for now. However, I suspect that what you've told us isn't the whole story!"

Chandra "I've shared everything I know. What I told you is all I'm aware of. If there's more, it's beyond what I can explain right now.", his throat tight with a mix of Guilt, relief, and lingering anxiety. The moon's light, now softer and less menacing, filtered through the small windows, casting a gentle glow over the chamber. The once oppressive atmosphere had given way to an uneasy peace.

Though the immediate danger seemed to have passed, Chandra's mind remained clouded with uncertainty. The night had taken its toll on him, leaving him emotionally and physically drained. He glanced at the cavemen, who were now sitting quietly, their energy spent. The chamber, though calmer, still held an air of residual tension, as if the night's horrors were not entirely finished.

As Chandra sat down, trying to steady his breathing, he reflected on the events that had transpired. The rituals had brought a temporary reprieve, but the weight of the night's experiences would linger. The full moon was still a day away, and the uncertainty of what lay ahead continued to gnaw at him.

The cavemen began to clean up the remnants of the ritual, their movements slow and deliberate. The once-chaotic energy of the chamber had settled into a sombre, reflective calm. Chandra's thoughts turned to his friends—those who had perished and those who had suffered. The haunting presence of Ananya, though seemingly pacified, left an indelible mark on the night.

The chamber, now bathed in a quiet, moonlit glow, held its secrets closely. The rituals had brought a temporary calm, but the scars of the night would remain. Chandra's resolve to confront the darkness and seek redemption for the suffering endured was unwavering. As the night stretched on, he knew that the full moon's arrival would bring its own challenges, and he steeled himself for whatever lay ahead.

Chapter 6– The Reckoning Tide

After performing the ritual, Chandra, tormented by the loss of his friends—Rakesh, Isha, and Bharat—returned home, desperately hoping that the worst was over. Exhausted and emotionally drained, he grappled with the weight of his grief and guilt. The nights were long and restless, filled with haunting memories and self-reproach.

It took Chandra over a week to begin the slow process of recovery, eventually leaving for Vizag as he could no longer bear to stay in that area. Despite his efforts to move on, the trauma of what had happened still haunted him. Seeking a distraction, Chandra arranged a date with a girl he matched with on Tinder. They met at a fancy restaurant, where he hoped the elegant surroundings might offer a brief escape from his inner turmoil.

As the girl walked in, Chandra couldn't help but notice her long hair, which reminded him of Ananya. Though still in a trance from his recent experiences, he tried to push the memories aside and focus on the moment. Forcing a smile, he cracked a few jokes, trying to distract himself and lighten the mood, even as his mind kept drifting back to the past.

As they enjoyed their meal, a waitress approached their table with a small, elegantly wrapped box. She handed it to Chandra, saying a girl had asked her to give it to him. Confused but intrigued, Chandra thanked her and opened the box, only to find a bottle of sleeping pills. His heart raced as a sense of dread washed over him. He quickly excused himself from the table, his mind racing as he drove home, the past week's events flashing through his mind.

Arriving home, Chandra's hands shook as he unlocked the door. He knew he had to confront the reality of his actions. As he arrived and began to piece together the memory of that fateful night, the events unfolded vividly in his mind.

That night, when Isha suggested going to the terrace, Rakesh went with her, followed by Chandra, who carried drinks. Chandra had secretly put slow-acting sleeping pills in all drinks. The effect of the pills became clear as Bharat and Rakesh soon fell into a deep sleep, their bodies collapsing on the ground from the alcohol and the pills.

In the haze of drunkenness, Chandra had taken the opportunity to act on his long-suppressed desires. He had made his way to Ananya's room, where both she and Isha were lying unconscious on the floor. Chandra, under the influence of his twisted impulses, had carefully lifted Ananya and placed her on the bed. He removed her clothes and began to kiss her including her most intimate areas and he forced himself on her. His actions were driven by a dark fantasy, convinced that she was simply asleep due to the pills he had administered.

The truth was far more horrifying than Chandra had imagined. In the days that followed, he learned that Ananya had been sexually assaulted by him while she was dead, and now, reflecting on that night with the full knowledge of the consequences, he realized that his actions had desecrated her in the most unimaginable way. He had violated not only her body but her memory, turning his deepest fears and regrets into a tragic reality. The weight of his actions, compounded by the knowledge of what had happened, became an unbearable burden as he faced the bleak truth of what he had done.

Chandra stumbled through the darkness, drenched in sweat and terror. The room he had just fled was shrouded in impenetrable blackness, amplifying the intensity of his fear. Suddenly, things started to fall, glass shattered, whispers filled the air, and a strong wind began to blow. Ananya's voice echoed through the void, each word dripping with cold, vengeful certainty.

"Did you think you could escape the Karma?"

Paralyzed by fear, Chandra's legs felt like lead as he struggled to move. He stumbled out of his bed, each step a battle against the overwhelming dread. His breath came in ragged gasps, his mind racing with images of what he had done. Desperation fuelled his flight as he raced through the empty streets, the night cloaked in a chilling silence that seemed to mock his terror. The weight of his sins dragged at every step, each breathe a reminder of his inescapable guilt.

Outside, Chandra's frantic sprint drew puzzled looks from passers-by, but no one could see the true source of his terror. To them, he appeared as just another man lost in a midnight drunk and panic, his actual fear invisible to those around him.

He reached the desolate beach, the roar of the waves mingling with his panicked breathing. The cold wind cut through him, amplifying his shivering. The moonlight, stark and unforgiving, illuminated the beach in an eerie glow. It was there that Ananya materialized before him, her presence a haunting spectre of sorrow and rage.

Her face, pale and illuminated by the moonlight, was a mask of anguish and fury. The sight of her was a dagger to Chandra's already tortured soul. He dropped to his knees, unable to escape the crushing weight of his actions.

"How can u do it to me?" Ananya's voice trembled with unshed tears, her words a haunting whisper that pierced through his guilt.

" If we can't trust those closest to us—our best friends, our Boyfriend, or even a female friend—then what value does a heart have? What good is it to beat if it's filled with such betrayal and deceit?"

Her gaze was unrelenting, her eyes filled with a blend of deep sorrow and unbridled rage. The memories of their time together flashed before Chandra's eyes: the laughter, the shared moments of joy, and the bitter betrayal of that fateful night. The vision of Ananya and Isha on the ground, incapacitated by the sleeping pills, haunted him with its haunting clarity. He recalled his own twisted thoughts and actions—the realization that he had acted on his darkest desires, believing Ananya to be asleep when she was actually a corpse.

Ananya's voice, filled with a supernatural force, broke through Chandra's chaotic thoughts. "You thought you could erase the pain and regret," she said, her voice echoing with a chilling certainty. "But the heart does not forget."

With a sudden, unearthly strength, she reached into his chest, tearing his heart from his body. Chandra's scream was a desperate wail, swallowed by the unfeeling night as the heart, now a gory symbol of betrayal, was cast into the void. The agony was excruciating, his life force draining away as Ananya's figure dissolved into the darkness, leaving him alone on the cold, empty beach where it all began and ultimately came to a tragic end.

As Chandra collapsed to the ground, his body lifeless and cold, the haunting echoes of his torment lingered in the night. The beach, once a place of solitude, was now a silent witness to the cruelty of his actions and the final, vengeful act of a soul wronged beyond measure.

***

Epilogue

Key Highlights

- **Silent Betrayal**: Even though Ananya discovered the affair at the party, she chose not to react immediately, Instead trying to piece together what was happening and whether Isha was complicit. Despite her unwavering belief that Bharat was her perfect, trustworthy partner as she even gave herself to him which girls do when they trust the most, her faith whole ,was obliterated when Isha revealed that Bharat had seduced her ,leaving Ananya disillusioned and emotionally numb. This revelation shattered Ananya's trust and left her emotionally paralyzed, underscoring the brutal reality of uncovering betrayal when you've been blind to the truth.
- **Backstab from Within**: Isha demonstrated that a girl can sometimes be her own greatest enemy. No matter how strong the friendship, there can come a time when someone backstabs you. No matter how deep the friendship, it can turn toxic, showing that shared experiences and supposed care mean nothing when backstabbing occurs.
- **Exposing Vulnerability**: Handing or allowing someone over private/personal items, including your mobile phone, which is now the definition of private in current era, exposes intimate details about your life and psychological state. Trusting anyone with such private information is a dangerous gamble, as it can leave you vulnerable to betrayal. Always be wary, as even your closest confidants can turn against you.
- **The Deception of Friendship**: You can never truly know someone, even if they are your greatest best friend

with loads of year's togetherness. Simply a mother may not fully know her son/daughter, a wife may not fully know her husband or vice versa, and a friend? Lets skip, no point of discussion here. Relationships start with care and emotional bonds, but lurking beneath the surface are hidden, darker desires waiting for the right moment to strike.

- **Karma's Retribution**: There is no such thing as a spontaneous action; everything is done with full awareness. While you don't need to be perfect, remember that karma will deliver its retribution. You are solely responsible for your actions, and there are no escapes from the consequences.

- **Facing Your Own Deception**: Victims of betrayal often deceive themselves as much as they are deceived by others. Accept your mistakes and recognize that you are not just a victim of others but of your own decisions. Life is a cycle of joy and pain, and understanding that you've invited trouble just as you've invited happiness is a harsh but necessary reality.

Final Reflection

As days pass by, it becomes increasingly apparent that trust is a fragile and evolving aspect of our lives. We often find it challenging to trust others with our private belongings, friendships, and even romantic relationships. Time changes people, and with it, the bonds we once held dear may dissolve or shift.

Losing a bond can be inevitable, but if a relationship persists without issues or conflicts, it might be worth questioning. Sometimes, enduring connections might mask underlying deceit. Reflect on your own relationships and consider: Is the trust you place in others truly reciprocal, or is there a hidden cost?

The author encourages everyone to embrace their one and only life fully, accepting both its triumphs and trials. Mistakes are a part of the journey—acknowledge them and accept your fate. If you find yourself a victim of betrayal or hardship, recognize it and move forward. Life is a continuous cycle of joy and struggle; both must be accepted. Dwelling on the past will only trap you; escape your troubles and be prepared for new challenges that lie ahead. But never let these obstacles stop you. Keep smiling, stay resilient, and press on with unwavering determination.

Feel free to share your Feedback or thoughts at saidurga52@gmail.com or on Instagram - @___son_of_krishna.

Acknowledgments

Thanks to Supporters

I would like to extend my deepest gratitude to all those who supported me throughout the writing of this book. Your encouragement, feedback, and unwavering belief in my vision were invaluable. Special thanks to my beta readers, whose insights and suggestions greatly enhanced the story.

About the Author

Gondesu Sai Durga Reddy is a passionate writer with a deep interest in exploring psychological and supernatural themes. With a background of a CA student, who draws on a rich web of experiences and influences to create compelling and thought-provoking stories. When not writing, he enjoys watching thrillers, which often inspire and enrich their writing. Sai Gindesu resides in Visakhapatnam, Andhra Pradesh, India, where they continue to craft stories that delve into the complexities of the human psyche.

Glossary

Key Terms and Concepts

- **Karma**: A concept referring to the principle of cause and effect where a person's actions, whether good or bad, influence their future.
- **Supernatural**: Elements beyond the natural world, often involving entities or forces or elements that defy scientific explanation.
- **Psychological Horror**: A genre that focuses on the mental and emotional state of characters, often exploring themes of Desires, fear, anxiety, and paranoia.
- **Manifestation**: The process by which abstract ideas or energies become tangible or visible, often associated with supernatural occurrences in the story.

www.ingramcontent.com/pod-product-compliance
Lightning Source LLC
Chambersburg PA
CBHW020456160726
47991CB00007B/2683

Table of Contents